D1317596

2

RECEIVED
OCT - 8 2008

By_____

HAYNER PUBLIC LIBRARY DISTRICT
ALTON, ILLINOIS

OVERDUES 10 PER DAY MAXIMUM FINE
COST OF BOOKS. LOST OR DAMAGED
BOOKS ADDITIONAL $5.00 SERVICE CHARGE.

BRANCH

Kane/Miller Book Publishers, Inc.

First American Edition 2008
by Kane/Miller Book Publishers, Inc.
La Jolla, California

First published in 2008 in Belgium by Pastel
Copyright © 2008, l'ecole des loisirs, Paris

All rights reserved. For information contact:
Kane/Miller Book Publishers, Inc.
P.O. Box 8515
La Jolla, CA 92038
www.kanemiller.com

Library of Congress Control Number: 2008921839
Printed and bound in China
1 2 3 4 5 6 7 8 9 10

ISBN: 978-1-933605-91-3

b18350768

Emmanuelle Eeckhout

There's
No Such Thing
as Ghosts!

Kane/Miller
BOOK PUBLISHERS

When we moved to our new neighborhood,
I had to promise my mother that I wouldn't
go near the strange old house on the corner.

"People say it's haunted," she whispered.

Haunted? There's no such thing as ghosts!

But if there is ... I'm going to catch one!

I opened the door and went inside.

There was no one on the stairs,

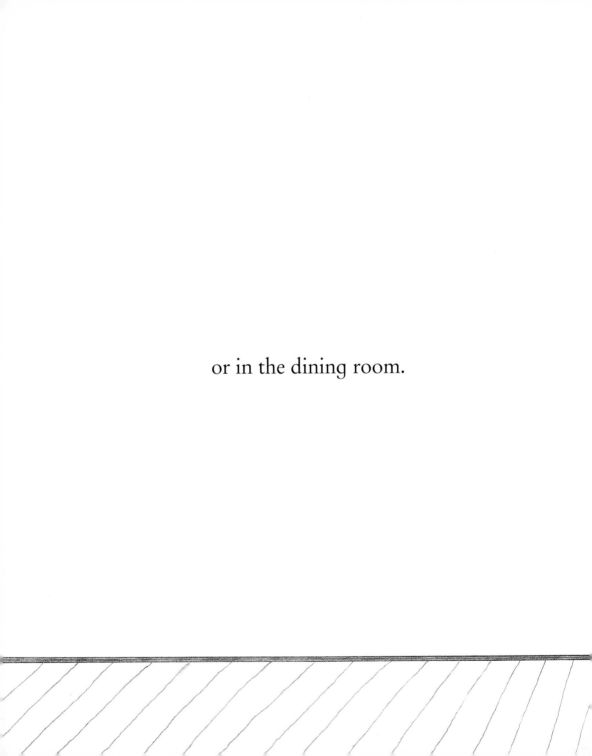

or in the dining room.

I searched the whole kitchen,
and didn't find anything.

I looked in the bedroom.

No one was there.

I checked the bathtub …

... nothing!

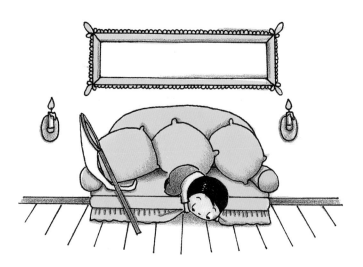

The living room was empty, too.

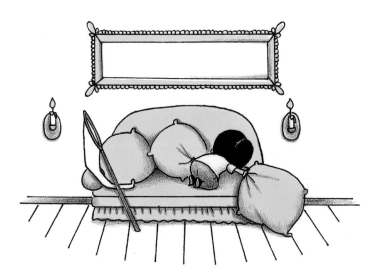

I looked very carefully.

The library was gigantic.
Who reads all these books?

I did find a secret passage,

but it was empty
(except for the spiders).

I searched everywhere!

I looked in every room.

This house isn't haunted.

I was right.

There's no such thing as ghosts!